THIS BEDTIME BOOK BELONGS TO

HEY DUGGEE

LADYBIRD BOOKS

UK | USA | Canada | Ireland | Australia | India | New Zealand | South Africa

Ladybird Books is part of the Penguin Random House group of companies whose addresses can be found at global.penguinrandomhouse.com.

www.penguin.co.uk   www.puffin.co.uk   www.ladybird.co.uk

 Penguin
Random House
UK

First published 2022
001

Text and illustrations copyright © Studio AKA Limited, 2022
Written by Lauren Holowaty

Printed in China

The authorized representative in the EEA is Penguin Random House Ireland,
Morrison Chambers, 32 Nassau Street, Dublin D02 YH68

A CIP catalogue record for this book is available from the British Library

ISBN: 978-1-405-95075-6

All correspondence to:
Ladybird Books, Penguin Random House Children's
One Embassy Gardens, 8 Viaduct Gardens, London SW11 7BW

DUGGEE   **DUGGLY**

THE BEDTIME BADGE

HAPPY   **BETTY**   **NORRIE**   **ROLY**   **TAG**

Duggee's nephew, Duggly,
is spending the day at
the clubhouse.
"Yay!" cheer the Squirrels.
They love it when Duggly
comes to visit.
"Hello, Duggly," says Betty.
"What do you want to
do today?"

In puppy talk, that means . . .

EVERYTHING!
"OK!" say
the Squirrels.

DO-DO!

MEOW!

BANG!

"Duggly looks a bit tired," says Norrie. "Maybe he has finished doing everything."

"Ah-woof," says Duggee.

After all that fun, it's Duggly's bedtime.

Uh-oh. Duggly doesn't like the word "bedtime".

Duggee picks up Duggly
to comfort him . . .

then puts him down
on a cushion.

"Duggee, it doesn't sound like Duggly wants it to be bedtime," says Tag.
Duggee thinks for a moment. Maybe Duggly needs a little help to go to sleep.
Luckily, Duggee has his **Bedtime Badge!**
He knows what to do.
"Phew!" The Squirrels sigh.

"Ah-woof-woof?" says Duggee. What makes you sleepy, Squirrels?

"Being outside makes me sleepy," says Happy dreamily.

RUNNING, SPLASHING . . .

Oh dear. It looks like Happy has nodded off.

WAKE UP, HAPPY. IT'S NOT YOUR BEDTIME!

ZZZZZ!

DUGGLY HAS ALREADY BEEN OUTSIDE TODAY.

AH-WOOF!

You're right, Betty.

"Ah-woof-woof?" says Duggee. What other things
make you sleepy, Squirrels?
"Cuddling teddy bears makes me sleepy," says Norrie.
"It makes me feel all cosy and warm."

The Squirrels give Duggly their teddies.
"Ahhhhh, Duggly!" cry the Squirrels.
He looks so cosy and warm and . . .

. . . awake!
Duggly giggles. He thinks the
Squirrels are playing a game.
He throws the teddies away.

Duggly, you're not
supposed to do that!

"Ah-woof-woof," says Duggee. Time to try something else. What other things make you sleepy, Squirrels?

MILK MAKES ME SLEEPY!

"Bedtime stories make me sleepy," says Betty. "Ah-woof!" says Duggee. That's a splendid idea, Betty! Why don't you read one to Duggly?

"Once upon a time, there was a unicorn," begins Betty. "She flew around the whole world, and she saw TEN different types of cloud. Altocumulus, altostratus . . ."

Duggly listens to Betty's story. He tries to keep his eyes open, but he's getting sleepy. He closes one eye, and then the other, and then . . .

"THE END!" shouts Roly.
Duggly is wide awake again!
"Oops!" says Roly.
"Nice one, Roly," says Norrie.
"Ah-woof-woof," says Duggee. Never mind.
That was a very good try.

WHAT MAKES YOU SLEEPY, TAG?

"Singing!" says Tag.
"Doesn't that keep you awake?" says Betty.
"Not if you sing like this," says Tag, and he starts to sing a lullaby in his quietest whisper.

LA LA, LA LA, LA LA . . .

Happy, Norrie, Betty and Roly join in with their quietest whispers.

They all sing the bedtime song together . . .

SINGING, SINGING TO SLEEP. IT'S A SLEEPY SONG.

SINGING, SINGING TO SLEEP. BED IS WHERE YOU BELONG.

SINGING, SINGING, "SLEEP TIGHT". THIS IS THE BEDTIME SONG.
SINGING, SINGING, "GOODNIGHT". YOU'LL BE ASLEEP BEFORE LONG . . .

Duggly's asleep at last! Well done, Squirrels. All that talking and singing about bedtime and feeling sleepy worked!

AHHH!

"Duggly looks so sweet sleeping," whispers Betty.

"Where's Duggee?" ask the Squirrels.

The Squirrels turn round to see Duggee snoring
in his chair!
Ah. It appears it's Duggee's bedtime too!
Well done, Squirrels. You've definitely earned
your **Bedtime Badges!**

Now there's just time for one last thing
before the Squirrels go home . . .

"DUGGEE HUG!"
whisper the Squirrels.